READING CORNER

A Bunch of Balloons

A humorous story
in a familiar setting

First published in 2004 by
Franklin Watts
96 Leonard Street
London
EC2A 4XD

Franklin Watts Australia
45–51 Huntley Street
Alexandria
NSW 2015

Text © Anne Cassidy 2004
Illustration © Philippe Dupasquier 2004

A CIP catalogue record for this book is available
from the British Library.

ISBN 0 7496 5743 X (hbk)
ISBN 0 7496 5781 2 (pbk)

Series Editor: Jackie Hamley
Series Advisors: Dr Barrie Wade, Dr Hilary Minns
Design: Peter Scoulding

Printed in Hong Kong / China

READING CORNER

A Bunch of
Balloons

Written by
Anne Cassidy

Illustrated by
Philippe Dupasquier

W
FRANKLIN WATTS
LONDON•SYDNEY

Anne Cassidy

"I love shiny balloons. I always buy as many as I can for my parties – just like the boy in my story!"

Philippe Dupasquier

"This book was fun to illustrate. I wonder how many balloons it would take to get me off the ground?"

It was the day of Joe's party.

5

Mum bought ten balloons.

"Hold these," she told Joe.

Joe held on tight, but there were just too many balloons.

Joe had to let four balloons go.

The wind blew and blew.

The wind tugged and tugged.

A balloon floated away.

A dog barked and Joe jumped.

Another balloon floated away.

"Hurry up, Joe!" said Mum.

"I'm coming!" said Joe.

But he left a balloon behind.

A bird pecked and a balloon
went BANG!

A baby cried and cried.

"Have this balloon!" said Joe.

Joe had only one balloon left.

But a fat cat was sitting on the fence and he popped it!

"Oh no! Where are all the balloons?" cried Joe's mum.

28

"No problem," said Joe's dad.

"I bought some balloons, too!"

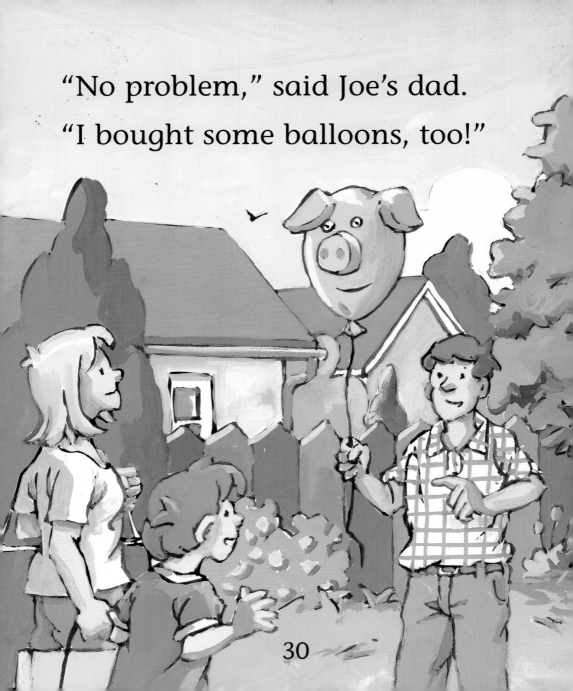

30

Notes for parents and teachers

READING CORNER has been structured to provide maximum support for new readers. The stories may be used by adults for sharing with young children. Primarily, however, the stories are designed for newly independent readers, whether they are reading these books in bed at night, or in the reading corner at school or in the library.

Starting to read alone can be a daunting prospect. **READING CORNER** helps by providing visual support and repeating words and phrases, while making reading enjoyable. These books will develop confidence in the new reader, and encourage a love of reading that will last a lifetime!

If you are reading this book with a child, here are a few tips:

1. Make reading fun! Choose a time to read when you and the child are relaxed and have time to share the story.

2. Encourage children to reread the story, and to retell the story in their own words, using the illustrations to remind them what has happened.

3. Give praise! Remember that small mistakes need not always be corrected.

READING CORNER covers three grades of early reading ability, with three levels at each grade. Each level has a certain number of words per story, indicated by the number of bars on the spine of the book, to allow you to choose the right book for a young reader:

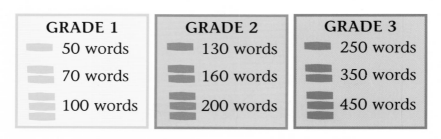

GRADE 1	GRADE 2	GRADE 3
50 words	130 words	250 words
70 words	160 words	350 words
100 words	200 words	450 words